GHOST CAT

EVE BUNTING and *Illustrated by* KEVIN M. BARRY

PUBLISHED BY SLEEPING BEAR PRESS

To Shane and Keelin. And Demo, too.
—Eve

❧

For Maui and Murphy
—Kevin

Sleeping Bear Press™

2395 South Huron Parkway, Suite 200, Ann Arbor, MI 48104
www.sleepingbearpress.com
© Sleeping Bear Press

Printed and bound in China.
10 9 8 7 6 5 4 3 2 1

Library of Congress Cataloging-in-Publication Data
Names: Bunting, Eve, 1928- author. | Barry, Kevin, 1981- illustrator.
Title: Ghost cat / written by Eve Bunting ; illustrated by Kevin M. Barry.
Description: Ann Arbor, MI : Sleeping Bear Press, [2017] | Summary: After
his death, Sailor Boy decided to stay at Port Carrick lighthouse with his friend,
the lighthouse keeper, and when disaster strikes, he is there to help.
Identifiers: LCCN 2017002861 | ISBN 9781585369935 (hard cover)
Subjects: | CYAC: Cats—Fiction. | Ghosts—Fiction. | Lighthouses—Fiction.
Classification: LCC PZ7.B91527 Ghd 2017 | DDC [E]—dc23
LC record available at https://lccn.loc.gov/2017002861

I'm a cat.
A **ghost** cat.
My name is Sailor Boy.

I live in the Port Carrick lighthouse with my friend,
Miss Maggie McCullen.
She has been the lighthouse keeper for many years.

I was her ordinary cat once, and when I passed away
I made my decision not to leave. So here I am.

The people in Port Carrick are proud of Miss Maggie.

"She keeps that big light going," they say.
"Never misses a night. Without her there'd be boats
smashed to pieces on the rocks. You can't count the lives
Miss Maggie and her light have saved."

Boats often pass close to the lighthouse and
sound their horns to thank her.

"Aye," the people of Port Carrick murmur,
"but it's a terrible lonely life she lives out there,
all by herself in that lighthouse."

They don't know about me, Sailor Boy.

I can be visible or invisible, whichever and whenever I choose.

It's fun!

I like daytimes in the lighthouse.

But I like nighttimes more. When the sun sets red on the horizon
and dusk drapes itself over the ocean our duties begin.

Miss Maggie and I climb the fifty steps,
round and round and round to the lighthouse tower.

She does all she needs to do to start the big beacon so that it shines its warning across the dark ocean.

I watch. I know it all by heart.

Miss Maggie pets me. "You could run this lighthouse by yourself, Sailor Boy. You're one smart cat."

I know.

Now and then we have visitors who pay
to see the lighthouse. Imagine!

I make myself **invisible** and tease them with
ghostly purrs or a little scratch at an ankle.
Sometimes I even tug on a shoelace till it comes loose
or drag a tissue out of an open purse.

Such fun to watch their faces!
If Miss Maggie sees, she frowns at me and I stop.

But one day a man stepped on my ghost tail and I let out a howl.

The visitors stared all around and someone said in a scared whisper,

"What was that?"

Miss Maggie calmed them.
"Oh, sometimes a crow lands on top
of the tower and screeches."
All was well again, except for my tail.

Time passes.

Visitors come and go.

Today Cissie Curry, a niece to
Miss Maggie, has come for a visit.

I thought she was a little foolish for I could see a storm
was brewing. She was to leave before dark but it's dark already
and the wind is screaming and the sea is snarling at the rocks.

Now she has to stay the night. I stay invisible.
Sometimes visitors make too much of a fuss over me.

"Cissie," Miss Maggie says, "it's time for me
to go up and light the light."

She leaves her niece at the kitchen fire with a cup of hot cocoa.
Then she and I hurry up the steps to the tower,
round and round and round.

But catastrophe!

In her haste Miss Maggie trips on step thirty and can't get up.

"It's my ankle," she groans. "It might be broken. Cissie!" she calls.
"Cissie, come and help me. Cissie! Cissie!"

But her niece can't hear through the shriek of the wind
and the battering of the waves.

I take a minute to comfort my friend, laying my face against hers.
Then I become visible and leap down all the steps to fetch Cissie.

"Oh my," she says, "I didn't know Aunt Maggie had a cat!"
She tries to pet me.

I have to make her understand what has happened.
I run to the steps and back, mewing as loudly as I can.
Run and come back. Run and come back.

Please, please, Cissie. Listen to what I am telling you.

At last she understands and follows me to the steps, up, up,
round and round and round.

She sees Miss Maggie. "Oh, Aunt Maggie!
Hold on to me. I will try to get you down."

But Miss Maggie gasps. "No! No, child!
Go up and light the beacon. There are lives at stake."

"I don't know how . . . ," Cissie begins.

But Miss Maggie's voice is now more forceful.
"Go! Sailor Boy will show you!"

"Your cat?"

"Yes."

I run ahead of her up the rest of the steps.
The lighthouse seems to rock in the gusts of wind.

The big beacon stands dark and still.

I know what to do.

I jump to where the matches are kept and then to the wick,
touching each with my paw. Back and forth. Back and forth.

Finally Cissie understands.

Hallelujah!

She lights the wick and the great beacon comes to life,
cutting through the dark night and shining out its warning beam.

"You're wonderful!" Cissie tells me.

I think she is, too.

We hurry down to see Miss Maggie.

"Is it lit?" she asks.

"It is," Cissie says.
"Now we'll take care of you."

In the kitchen she wraps cold rags on Miss Maggie's ankle.
The wind blasts around the walls and Cissie has to shout.

"Soon as the storm has passed I'll go fetch Dr. Smith.
And I can stay for a while and look after you and the light.
Now that your extraordinary cat has shown me how.
But I don't see him. Where is he?"

"Oh, he's around." Miss Maggie smiles at invisible me.
"Sometimes he just likes to disappear."

I suppose maybe I am **extraordinary**.

But who wants to be ordinary?

AUTHOR'S NOTE

Lighthouses are towers with beacon lights and are built near the shores of large lakes and oceans. The bright light warns ships and other watercraft of hazards ahead. The hazards might be sharp rocks or hidden reefs, which could sink a ship if not seen in time. Before there were lighthouses, people on shore lit huge warning fires that they hoped could be seen by ships at sea. How many lives and how many ships have been saved by lighthouses? The number cannot be counted.

Lighthouse keepers–men, women, or families–lived in small houses nearby or in quarters within the tower. They were responsible for keeping the beacon light lit. It was a lonely life, filled with never-ending work. Thunder, lightning, gale-force winds that rocked the tower could not stop them from their duties. The light must never fail.

In the beginning the light came from candles; then in the 1870s from lamps fueled first by whale oil, then by kerosene. Later, electricity was used. Several improvements in "the lamp," as the beacon was called, came during the 1800s. The gas "crocus" burner, invented by John Richardson Wigham, produced light that was thirteen times stronger and more brilliant than any light ever seen before. And the Fresnel lens, invented in 1822, allowed the light to be seen from an even greater distance.

Technology in modern times has brought more changes. Now the lamp in the tower is automatic and there is no need of a lighthouse keeper. But the old stories are remembered. Stories of lighthouse keepers who rowed out in their small dinghies to save drowning sailors. Stories of ice and snow that marooned keepers for months on end.

Many lighthouses still stand, maintained in the United States by the US Coast Guard. They fascinate landlubbers. Some have been changed into bed-and-breakfast lodgings. The visitor can lie in bed and watch the lamp sweep across the dark ocean as it had probably done for more than two hundred years.

A few years ago my husband and I saw an ad in an Irish newspaper: LIGHTHOUSE FOR SALE. We were excited. The lighthouse was on the northern coast of Ireland, facing the Irish Sea with its storms and crashing waves. But alas, someone else bought it before we could. So sad! We might even have found a ghost cat in residence!

Sleep well! And imagine!